The Best Mum

PENNY HARRISON SHARON DAVEY

NEW FRONTIER PUBLISHING

My friends have the BEST mums.
I'm hoping I might trade.
They're *never* late for anything.
They know each kind of braid.

The Best Mum

For all the best mums, including my own – Dotti and Tri.
(And for Rebecca, of course, who really is amazing.) – P H

To Neve and Alex, always – S D

First published in the UK in 2021
by New Frontier Publishing Europe Ltd
Uncommon, 126 New King's Road, London, SW6 4LZ
www.newfrontierpublishing.co.uk

A CIP catalogue record for this book
is available from the British Library.

ISBN: 978-1-913639-62-4 (PB)

Designed by Verity Clark

Printed and bound in China
1 3 5 7 9 10 8 6 4 2

Katie's mums are wizards
At dress-up days for school.

They snip and sew into the night,
With feathers, lace and tulle.

My mum makes
my costumes

With sticky tape

and glue.

She **grunts** and **mutters** to herself,

'Well, that'll have to do.'

Scout's mum is amazing.

She even rollerskates.

She can swish and glide, just like a swan,

Into a figure eight.

My mum tried to **skate** once.
She was like a baby deer.

She

wibble-wobbled

on her **feet**

While everyone kept clear.

Jai's mum is a **pop** star.

She always sings along.

She **disco-dances**
on a chair
To every latest song.

My mum likes the opera.
She says it keeps her calm.

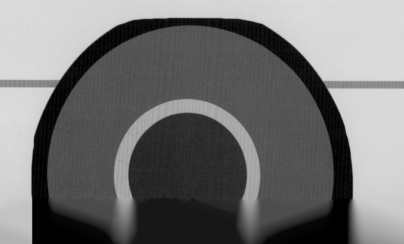

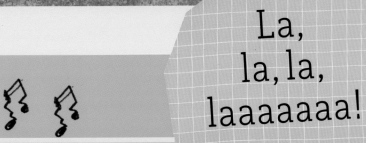

But when she tries to sing along,
It's like our car alarm.

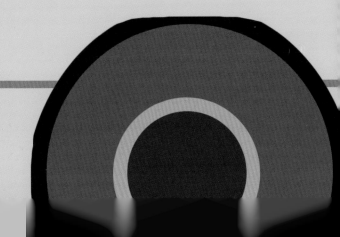

Eve's mum is a fairy.

I've even seen her wings.

She flutters through the playground

In her sparkly skirts and rings.

My mum doesn't flutter.

She *scrambles* out the gate.

Will's mum is a **top chef**
When cooking snacks and treats.

She makes sushi for his lunchbox,
And rare, **exotic** sweets.

And when I open up my lunch
There's *always* something **icky**.

Huy's mum is an athlete.
She stretches at first light.

She hikes and bikes at weekends
And meditates each night.

My mum likes to sleep in.

Zzzzzz!

When she runs, she gets a stitch.

And if she tries to meditate
Her left eye starts to twitch.

My friends have the best mums.
But mine will do just fine. . .

Cos when she **cuddles** me each night
I'm kind of glad she's mine.